I0762248

The

Sky Angels

A novella.

Colin E Wells

Cover illustration by Bex Sutton at Primal Studios

This is a work of fiction and no offence is meant by the content herein, although the historical data is evidentially correct at the time of writing.

Foreword

In the industrial age of the 19th Century during the reign of Queen Victoria, the land changed, raped of its natural wonders and manipulated beyond all recognition. Only very small pockets of the once green and pleasant land remain in the Royal Forest of Dartmoor in Dumnonia, and in Cumberland.

The once great and resplendent Kingdom of Jórvík and what was Mercia is now a maze and mass of heavy industry, mining and milling, the once great green hills and dales once raped and pillaged by the Vikings now being raped and pillaged by greedy fat-bellied businessmen, with no time of day for history. The land now confined to soot, slag, coal and waste brought about by supplying Londinium with the provision to make the capital prosper.

Londinium itself was rebuilt heavily after the great Fire of 1666 and then re-invented during the reign of Queen Victoria into a sprawling undignified metropolis. However, the great fire of 1666 was not the first "great" fire to devastate Londinium. The first recorded one was in 60 AD during Queen Boudica (meaning Victory) and her Celtic Iceni tribe uprising and revolt again the Roman overlords, prior to the

Queen killing herself to avoid capture as per the text of Tacitus or dying of illness as written by Cassius Dio. Then again in 122 AD during Emperor Hadrian's reign and 675 AD which destroyed the Saxon cathedral. Smaller fires took hold in 798 AD, 982 AD and 989 AD, although all of these linked to the timber constructed buildings. A major fire occurred in 1087 which destroyed St Paul's Cathedral and most of the Norman city. Before 1666, the phrase "Great Fire of London" was generally used by Londoners to denote one of two major conflagrations in the early medieval period. The first blaze occurred on Pentecost Sunday 26 May 1135, and the second occurred on Tuesday 10 July 1212., the latter starting in Southwick on the south side of the Thames and causing the deaths of three thousand Londoners as the fire took hold and spread across London bridge.

The Great Fire of 1666 which started in Pudding Lane displaced some seventy thousand of the eighty thousand Londoners, however only six deaths were actually recorded one of these being the maid of Thomas Farriner, in whose baker's house the fire started just after midnight on Sunday 2 September.

The metropolis of London during the reign of Queen Victoria consisted of exclusivity and wealth in the West and absolute poverty in the East, the only common nauseating factor between the two being the combination of coal-fired stoves and poor sanitation which made the air heavy and foul-smelling. Immense amounts of raw sewage were dumped straight into the Thames River running along gulleys and verges from both sections of the community before the invention and creation of 1400 miles of tunnels and pipes to take the excrement from the streets, underground.

On the surface the new cult of Vampyrism took hold and those supposedly bitten by a creature of the night. The charismatic and sophisticated vampyre of modern fiction was born with the publication of The Vampyre by John Polidori in 1819. This story was highly successful and arguably the most influential vampyre work of the early 19th century, almost one hundred years before Bram Stoker wrote Dracula. These night creatures roamed the night rubbing shoulders with the rich and poor preying on the young, the virginal and anyone else who they fancied to take part in their strange mystical ritualistic dark and forbidden practices, which were widely frowned upon by the establishment as a whole.

But underground it was different the Dashwood's Hellfire Club had reformed and started its secretive practices under the motto "Fais ce que tu voudras" or simply "Do what thou wilt" but not under the infamous riot causing Sir Francis Dashwood who in 1763 raised a tax on cider before immediately resigning as Chancellor of the Exchequer and taking a seat in the burgeoning House of Lords taking the title Baron Le Despencer. The new owner was a distant relative to the first Abbot and was an equally influential member of the upper class delightfully bringing back the dark practices from a century before.

The rich got richer and the poor just died in squalid conditions, paupers' graves springing up all over the east end of Londinium and out along the Thames Estuary as far as the eye could perceive. There was no middle ground and the great class divide was evident in as much as the perversion of justice and religion, the key was prosperity, wealth and status. And therein lay the absolute problem with Victorian society.

This my dear reader is only a snapshot of Victorian Londinium to give you a flavour of the scene. Although occasionally one may if they were extremely lucky see a Dragon fly through the sky being chased by or chasing a Dirigible firing everything including broken shards of the very heavy Belfast kitchen sink or tin bath.

Chapter One – The beginning

The dirigible hummed slowly over the coast-line of Kernow, the persistent low dark cloud cover masked its approach to the border of the, what was green and pleasant land. Below, the black tin mines stood resolute in the sky bleaching their acrid smoke, polluting the sky and the land.

The large hydrogen filled ship pressed further eastwards, bouncing over the smoke stacks of the chimneys of the area surrounding Penzance, the tiny port of Falmouth up to St Austell, then across the south of the county, following the well-worn smugglers' paths onward along the coast to Plymouth and the new Laira re-fuelling station before the trip to Exeter and beyond. Beyond to the metropolis that was Londinium, the un-holy smoke. Usually the journey took them from Plymouth, along the coaching roads, through the small villages of Ivybridge, South Brent, passing the village of Buckfastleigh with its ruined Cistercian Abbey and skirting other unusually sounding place names to the city of Exeter, its cathedral and a final overnight stopping point before the long journey to the Metropolis. Only this time they took a more direct route from Plymouth, heading north easterly in a relative straight line toward Exeter over the moor, where the air was sweet and clean. Diverting only in their flight path to pay service to the Cross of Childe before zig-zagging to the Church of St Michael at Brentor and then on to Bowerman's Nose high on the moor.

The County of Devon fast approached and with it the green, green grass of their home, untainted by industry. Too long had they only seen the blue and the black, the sea and the sky, nought that night time was upon them, just the smelt from the shallow and deep tin mines both along the southern rugged coast and more inland areas of Kernow but now as they approached the moor their vista was lit with sunlight and a green/brown hue of the moorland.

The Dartmoor National Park with its cragged rocks and rolling rivers in valleys of green and brown. Even then ponies roamed the moor, majestic in their surroundings enjoying the freedom; sheep covering the lowlands and path ways. Proper civilisation had failed to conquer this outland but small pockets grew out of the farming and with it small villages. Each village housing its own ale house, brewing its own unique tipple and a small Wesleyan Chapel or Church. Many surrounded and shrouded with superstition; headless horses and coachmen, hairy hands and of course the obligatory black dogs or wishthounds, which a prolific writer would take to heart during a bout of illness and turn into a best seller.

High to the south western part of the Moor the north winds blew an icy blast across her face as she stood at the open door of their vast sprawling manor house to the formal gardens, the wind as if calling to her; beckoning her to follow into the dark satanic night, away from the safety of the warm and welcoming if not eerie mansion that she knew as home. A home albeit alone save a wolf, her familiar and her companion and in the stillness of the cool evening a long low howl vibrated and carried on the stiffening breeze. A noise liken to a warning to both the living and the dead to stay away.

Writers note – The first recorded airships/dirigibles in Plymouth were towards the end of the First World War at RNAS Laira where two Sea Scout Rigid Airships were based, supporting the anti-submarine patrols based at RNAS Cattewater. RNAS Cattewater being the home to seaplanes and flying boats during the conflict, before being commission as RAF Cattewater in 1918 with the formation of the RAF Cattewater, which changed its name and status to RAF Mount Batten in 1928 and became one of the principal bases for the RAF Marine Branch, home of the Type Two HSL (Whalebacks). The RAF Marine Branch was then re-named as RAF Search and Rescue Force during the Second World War utilising the HSL along with Short Sunderland and Catalina flying boats until 1986, when the base was decommissioned and faded into obscurity.

Chapter Two - Land of Armanthian

The rider lay on the carpet of red and yellow dusty leaves, he had not seen nor been this way before. His large noble beast lay beside him, brought down by something not of their world, a glamour maybe or a poison in the air, they will never know. The one question was; could it be that both dragon and rider were alive.

The air around them was not the pleasant of odours but it was bearable, the dragon's flame was extinguished and the odour was the dragon's breath or at least the last remains of the fire-breath. Exhausted the rider pulled himself away from the dragon, his charge and badly wounded he passed out, never before had he been on the receiving end of dragon's fire breath. His Anmegil under his side, long since blooded with the blood of his enemies and now covered in his blood, his armour albeit a chain shirt had no protection to the razor edge of the tempered blade. The cut was clean and slowly healing but he lay there not wanting to disrupt the process, so slept. Waking from what seemed to be an eternity …weakly he called to his dragon, nothing, he called again, nothing, and thrice he called, the dragon's eyes flickered; it was alive but motionless save the fire-breath. Only minutes had passed since they were overhead on route to the Priory Keep of Armanathian at the request of the Abbot.

Focusing what little vision he had left he saw a figure in white coming towards him gracefully, the long dress trailing, the blonde hair flowing. Cautiously he reached for his side blade, it was gone, probably lost during the dragon's free-fall so he resigned himself to whatever fate the great creator had in store for him that day as he passed out for the second time that day. Beauty knelt beside him wiping his brow with the tail of her dress, lovingly and deftly healing him of his injuries…there was nothing she could do for the dragon save taking the egg that the noble fire breathing beast bore but the rider, the rider she let sleep, whilst she drifted back into the shadows from whence she came, vanishing completely.

As the black soot strangled the earth, nothing and nobody stood in its way, fire had ravaged even the parts that fire could not travel, corpses lay upon corpses as the earth groaned under the dead bleaching into the soil; and oh, how the moon cried as its light tried to shine through the vail of blackened clouds.

The whole earth had died, and last remnants of life had retreated underground or into the deepest caves away from the carrion and surviving scavengers, taking with it the last bastion of hope; an egg and within the egg a saviour of the living age; a dragon.

The last Dragon-keeper nursed the egg between her soft warm hands; whilst inside the dragon grew, feeding on the liquid in the sack and in the warmth of her hands and of her voice. A bond was being formed between the two and naught should rent them asunder. The jewel in her headpiece glowed softly providing light, a soft welcoming light into the gloom. Her staff resting against the corner of the cave but within arms' reach with her saddle. Her white horse long since gone to the otherworld.

In the corner of the cave slept her draug, as white as snow in winter, naught that snow could be remembered. This draug was her familiar; as she protected the egg so the draug protected her.

She knew it would soon be time for the dragon to break free of the confines of its surroundings and breathe for the very first time. Beside the egg in the nest lay a stack of small rodents, mice mainly although the odd rat did creep into the equation and thrown away as the land was still poisoned. Each mouse was fresh each day and then discarded upon the sound of the division bell that heralded a new day as the moon reached its zenith and the sun or rather what was left of the sun decline to its zenith on the far side of the world, and hopefully the birth of a new saviour.

But yesterday was not the day, neither is today, and probably not tomorrow, nor even the day after that as the moon was now on the wane and the new moon not due for a few days hence. The new moon signalled the arrival of newness, a new birth; the old guard, the blood guard having passed during the last twenty-eight days and a new guard in preparation for the forthcoming.

Even in the confines of the sancturific cave she knew the old guard had gone into passing as the days became fresher and the sky albeit still black became a softer almost grey-black. The middle summer was fast approaching and with it coincided the new moon over Armanthian, the sacred place in the land of the living not unlike Valhalla or Heaven, on the ancients' holy day of Faradome, the summer solstice and the feasting day of St John the Baptist. Neither Pagan nor Christian was she; she was the last of her kind, last of the old ways where myth and magic lurked with swords and dragons, hidden from the light save for her face and hands she was a healer, a fallaner and a warrior, an ohtar, the Queen of her, of her people long forgotten and long since gone west and having found eternal sleep, one of the Nandaror.

Only the ghosts of her vast family surrounded her now as she nursed this egg, this most precious of all the Creator's creations, this nameless saviour.

This, this gold dragon, the mal'loki.

An eerie mist hovered low across the valley, the lake surrounded by the hills itself was tumbling with a white ghost whilst high in the sky the mythical and mystical beasts circled, riding the thermals, that came off the hills, high, watching and waiting for the kill that never came.

Slowly from the grey-green water the glint of an object arose, followed by a second as the clouds parted and allowed a shaft of glorious white light to fall from the heavens to the water below. The pommel of a sword rose, followed by a handle lifted high by two fair hands, then the tang and blade. As the long sword got higher the hands took hold of the blade and tilted it towards the light. The mist and the beasts disappeared, save the rolling white ghost on the surface. The shore was awash with white before the green of the Albion grass began to poke its way through into the light. Small tufts and mounds appeared as if marking and reclaiming ground. And with that passing the sword glided slowly beneath the surface, waiting to be re-claimed by the one.

And so a king is born and thus begins the tale of Pendragon and Avalon...it was the time of the pre-dark ages when Albion was divided into smaller kingdoms, even before the formation of Wessex, Mercia and their ilk...Celtic tribes ruled the north and far south west, the Vikings had most of middle what was to become this sacred isle of Albion, our home.

For our tale takes place centuries hence, long after Arthur laid claim to the sword and united the nations before being injured upon the field of battle at the Battle of Camlann in the year of our Creator 537AD and returning to Avalon to be healed and eventually pass to the afterlife. The sword taken by Sir Griflet who on the trice time of asking by the mortally wounded Arthur, casts Excalibur into the lake whereupon the lady of the lake catches the sword and draws it to waters below.

The midnight black stallion carried his Queen far into the night as the Saxon hordes swept over Albion. Arthur, the once great bringer of peace to the land was gone but soon a king will come and the Sword of Avalon, the defender of Albion; the Excalibur will rise once more but until that time she would try and claim it for her own. Lady Morgana would be Queen, even for a day of all Albion. She would need Excalibur, whence returned by Sir Griflet to the mystic lake in the west, returned to the Lady of the Lake in Avalon, her Avalon, her home as one of the nine sisters. Excalibur would do her bidding, hers to wield, that great anmegil' in a world was no longer sorglas, she had seen to that, neianor was over it was her time. The time of the Queen. It was hrive and the ice was thick, the lake frozen, the air cold, all along the hills the remains of the still burning fires of Beltane lit up the dark inky sky...the moon had not been seen since Arthur's death, perhaps this was an omen, perhaps darkness had descended upon the land, perhaps good will come to the land. Only the Creator would know and that knowledge would naught be passed to such of the wizards of land. Merlin had gone and with it the old ways had gone to; only she remained of the once noble house of Pendragon, albeit adopted as a promise by Uther to Igraine, following the death of Lady

Morgana's father Gorlois in battle whilst the couple laid together.

Pendragon, even the name in itself evokes passion but that was in the past and this was now Lady Morgana's time and the land would either bleed or heal under her rule. As she gathered pace towards the waters, the ice began to crack and the blade of kings rose from the black depths of that mystical place, her sceptre isle, her home before descending back to the depth until a worthy successor was able to possession of that great symbol of rule.

Years nee decades later and far away in a broken rain soaked mud infested clearing, a triple shot from his wine skin usual settled him down, he didn't want to visit that place again but it was over and hopefully the last time anything like that would happen. His mind wandered back and forth as he sat there sharpening the long sword that had been at his side from his investiture all those years before. It had been blooded on more than one occasion but this was different, this was about love and honour; his love for his lady, the one who brought him happiness whom he would protect even if it meant laying down his own life.

He patched up his wounds like so many times before only with age the healing process took longer and age withered him. It would soon be time to pass the blade back to the maiden of the lake for safe-keeping until another one, another loremaster befitting the status was able to draw the sword and re-unite the lands. Only then would he pass over into eternal sleep and peace. But for now he surveyed the lands that lay bleeding and his own heart bled. His horse standing beside; tall and proud, ready to carry his master to battle or the worlds' end.

As the years passed the land became more and more rebellious, Monarchs came and went and it was time for the warrior, the Loremaster to retire to the safe haven of Armanthian in the west, the green isle of his fore-fathers and the great sword returned to the lake from whence it came until another was worthy to take the hilt and raise it aloft in the name of the Creator. In the intervening years many had searched and many had died looking for the Sword of Kings, this Caliburn, this Excalibur; the sacred lake not ready to reveal its secret to a world that was not ready. However, one day a worthy king will come and thrice the sword will once more rise to be taken from the watery depths of Avalon or moreover his haven.

Chapter Three - Tenna' ento lye omenta........

As the black soot strangled the earth, nothing and nobody stood in its way, fire had ravaged even the parts that fire could not travel, corpses lay upon corpses as the earth groaned under the dead bleaching into the soil; and oh how the moon cried as its light tried to shine through the vail of blackened clouds and the north winds blew an icy blast across her face as she stood at the open door of her family seat since 1700 to the walled formal gardens. The wind calling to her; beckoning her to follow into the dark satanic clear night, away from the safety of the warm and welcoming if not eerie mansion that she knew as home. A home albeit alone save a familiar. Her family had long since departed along with the serving staff, leaving just a bare shell, the furniture covered in old white drapes as if shut up for the season; when Londinium beckoned. For the last few months she had been living out of her travel trunk, whilst she gathered her thoughts. Her parents had departed whilst she was at finishing school in Europe and she had not been allowed to return home for the funeral; and the family expressly forbade daguerreotype, post-mortem photographs allowing loved ones to remember their dead relatives so all she had where her memories and the heavy damask covered contents of the mansion, her legacy.

She allowed the wind to carry her into the gloom, as an icy chill fell around and about her. Wrapping the shawl around her tightly she was carried over the formal gardens and down to the lake, upon which a weak reflection of the moon floated, casting little light towards a fallen branch beckoning her to sit.

Alone she sat on the branch of the old tree, its branches bowing to the water that passed beneath it, the tips gracefully tickling the ripples. As she waited, her thoughts wandered, remembering how and why she had ended up looking overlooking the tidal lake as the darkness of night enveloped the day. What was it her father said in the past, something about wandering off, staying close to home, not going down to the lake. Well she'd done all three. She'd be in trouble when she got home, she felt like that child again and soon to be her ageing ceremony, the time when she was no longer a child but ready to serve her Lord or Lady, whichever she was to be assigned to. But she did not want to become of age, she as the youngest wanted to remain a child, forever the child, the laito, her nickname. Everyone in the village called her Laito, Laito this and Laito that and she hated it; hated it with a passion wondering if they even knew her real name. Quietly she slid off the branch into the cool lake, once more.

As she stayed beneath the surface allowing the cold water to envelop her body a silver moon crept out from behind the blackening clouds, parting the gloom and enlightening the valley floor below bathing it in a shimmering light enveloping the beauty that lay before. High on the hill in the shadow of the moon stood a lonely black figure, normally beautified in swathes of bright colour, but cursed by night, the colours turned to jet black allowing it to become a silhouette in the night's sky, tall and proud, dark and foreboding. The silver moon cut a swathe of light upon the lake in the bottom of the garden; its clear crystal waters reflecting back a perfect image of the night sky. Even the stars were now visible upon that magical night, the night of Faelvrin. How Faelvrin even came to be in that area was a mystery but what was meant to be and was meant to pass is the Great Creator had written in the scrolls of history and confined to the annuls of time.

Bending down the beautiful pure white animal drank from the lake, casting a shadow upon the water unlike nothing before…pure, innocent and magical, the stars peering from behind the inky clouds as if bowing down to this, this beauty. Free and unbound, Faelvrin would know only freedom and ultimately companionship, but that is for another day; for now, Faelvrin raised her head and turned towards the mountains behind her, disappearing into the darkness.

As she surfaced back into the gloomy night sky, she forgot about the ageing ceremony so long ago; tonight she was re-born nee baptised under the light of a silver moon and a noble unicorn's gaze. She came from that Ranger stock, albeit not that she knew but tonight the Assassin was ready. The Assassin was born.

Chapter Four - The Assassin – Londinium 1850

Just at the turn of the half century in the thirteenth year of the reign of her sovereign majesty Queen Victoria; the darkness fell as she crouched low with her mechanical wings folded flat; the steam turbine bleaching warm air noisily muffled her approach to the edge of the roof and her decent to her quarry below.

Like Icarus before her she wanted to fly but unlike Icarus it was not just a quick prayer to the Gods and a leap of faith. She knew how to fly and her mechanical wings enabled her to stalk her prey easily and silently. For all intents and purposes at several hundred feet she looked just like a swallow-tailed bird of prey and that's how she liked it and that's how it remained.

But for now she was on the ground albeit ten floors up, preparing, her flamed strawberry hair perched high on her crown and allowed to fall in waves around her pretty Elven face, which sparked the question, dear reader, how could one so pretty be so dangerous. She stretched her wings and felt the freedom to fly, a pair of recently developed and prototype 1851 Colt Navy 44's strapped to her side, the barrels being shortened to accommodate her dainty figure and to allow a quicker exit, the bore having been filed to remove the rifling and signature of the cartridge. Her watch held high on her upper arm ticked down to a virtually audible alarm. It was time. With that she made her way to the edge, adjusted her brass goggles and jumped. Freefalling for what seemed like an age, she rode the thermals from the street below. Up and down but always just out of recognition by the hundreds of rats below. If she had been a real bird of prey it would have been a killing frenzy; lunch everywhere. But this time the rats could scurry all they wanted in the soot and smog that hovered between the once crisp sandstone and concrete buildings. As she rode the thermal updrafts she momentarily lost herself in the mid-day sun that shone down on her before she became obscured. A quick break in the thermals and a sudden drop brought her back to her senses especially as she spied her target. Not that she could miss him, the target stood at around seven foot without his boots on and was almost as broad, an easy target. Soft and fleshy. With her target in her sights she pulled the silent trigger. The projectile sped towards its intended recipient and as it did she banked and disappeared out of sight. If anyone looking in her general direction would have seen the silhouette of a large falcon looking for prey on the thermals.

On the sidewalk lay a corpse, blooded from the cartridge exploding in the chest, another faceless victim to be identified only by the tattoos on what was left of the oversized arms and the charcoaled clothing. Blackened blood and sinew sliding slowly into the newly built drainage system. Another criminal executed. Another undesirable off the streets of this her Londinium. Only this was her first of many.

Allowing time to enjoy the free-flight she made her way back to her jump site. Landing safely on the roof she peered over the parapet and smiled, before emptying the contents of her stomach over the roof taking care not to get covered. Correcting herself she removed her wings and goggles and stored them safely away before beginning to return to the office below, as if nothing had happened and back to the mundane life as a secretariat's assistant. In other words, a "glorified "slave but it served a purpose and kept her looking outwardly respectable. A young Victorian lady. Adjusting her skirt and bustle and tiding her hair into a tight bun she opened the door and made her way down the newly installed staircase to her floor, where she slipped behind her desk as if nothing had happened. Her weaponry and accessories secreted in the folds of her over-sized and over-boned skirt, hidden from view but equally accessible. Even her matching parasol, one of many matching her clothing, harboured a secret that none but her and the manufacturer knew about and she hoped that no-one never would.

Her first assignment was complete and would be deemed a success by her superiors whom she had never met. How did she become involved in such a covert group known as Harpers or Nandaror.

This was the Victorian semi-secret re-incarnation of Guild of Harpers. Harper agents are the "field agents" of the Harper organization, acting directly to gather intelligence and eliminate threats to the greater good. The greater good in this era being Her Majesty, Queen Victoria and her consort Prince Albert, the British Empire and her Creator. The Harpers were an old organization that had risen, been shattered, and risen again several times over the centuries. Its longevity and resilience are largely due to its decentralized, grassroots, secretive nature, and the near-autonomy of many of its members. The Harpers have “cells” and lone operatives throughout Faerûn, although they interact and share information with one another from time to time as needs warrant. Although some members worked cell-like but these were mainly non-field operatives, the secret backroom staff. The Harpers' ideology is noble, and its members pride themselves on their integrity and incorruptibility. Harpers do not seek power or glory, only fair and equal treatment for all.

Harper agents are trained to act alone and depend on their own resources. When they get into scrapes, they don't count on their fellow Harpers to rescue them. Nevertheless, Harpers are dedicated to helping one another in times of need, and friendships between Harpers are nigh unbreakable. Masterful spies and infiltrators, they use various guises and secret identities to form relationships, cultivate their information networks, and manipulate others into doing what needs to be done.

Although most Harpers prefer to operate in the shadows, there are exceptions to that rule but not in Londinium.

However, this reincarnation of the Guild of Harpers was more akin to an Assassins Guild albeit sanctioned by the leaders at the top. The beliefs of the guild did not change from ancient time and were threefold being that "One can never have too much information", that "Too much power leads to corruption", and that "No one should be powerless" and it was by those beliefs she lived her day, evening and night time existence. She was a Harper with a duty to perform. A duty to cleanse for the greater good of humanity.

As she left the confines of the office block, having bade the concierge a good evening she made her way through the inner courts towards her lodgings on the north side of the Thames. Not her favorite place but a chance to rest, although she would never call it home. Her home was a white cottage in Dumnonia, affectionately known as Avalon. Her Avalon, her sacred isle in the bleak and corrupted country. A white cottage on the blind side of the road to the prison, hidden from view by the walls of the foreboding empty building save a few tradesmen keeping the buildings serviceable.

After a light meal she slowly drifted off to sleep, listening to the sounds of the church bells, her head filled with dreams of home, her parents and her pet, although now a little larger than a domestic pet, even larger than a horse and the tiny Church on the top of the hill overlooking both the cottage and the newly re-instated prison. The Prison built on Duchy land owned by the Prince of Wales to house French and American prisoners during the Napoleonic campaign who at the time where anchored in prison hulks in Plymouth Sound at least a day's route march from where the prison was built. However, once the surviving prisoners of war where re-patriated in 1816, the prison fell into silence until 1850 when owing to an increase in populous and criminality it was repaired, rebuilt and opened as a general maximum secure prison. The 1841 census it showed that only a few workers remained on site keeping the buildings functional. There were reports of "gas" being produced from the peat bogs around but the records are sketchy and sealed for eternity.

Her sleep never lasted long as her dreams interrupted the sleep pattern and she found it better to awaken and prepare herself for the day that lay there trying to return to a sleep that never came. Those lonely hours before the dawn she spent cleaning her guns and calibrating her watch for the day ahead, should she be called to service.

Following her successful first mission she was called upon again; the next assignment was a few weeks later and this time she crouched low behind the same wall, her mechanical wings folded flat. The same steam turbine bleaching warm air noisily muffling her silent approach to the edge of the roof and her decent to her quarry below.

She knew how to fly, having spent the intervening period practicing in secret when the skies were quiet; when dirigibles couldn't fly at night thus making the mechanical wings almost noise free which enabled her to stalk her prey easily and silently. For all intents and purposes at several thousand feet she looked just like a swallow-tailed bird of prey and that's how she liked it and that's how it remained until the passing of the division bell that heralded the dawn of a new decade.

As she ritually prepared, her flame red hair perched high on her crown and allowed to fall in waves around her pretty Elven face, pretty but oh so dangerous. The same Colt '44 nestled safely in her tiny hand. It was time. With that she made her way to the edge, adjusted her brass goggles and jumped, allowing the updraft to lift her rigid wings taking her into the dark foreboding skies. Flight became her and after searching the gloom she eventually spotted her quarry. With her target in her sights as she pulled the silent trigger. The silent hammer fell against the cartridge and the projectile sped towards its intended recipient and as it did she floated to a thermal vent and pulled up sharply disappearing out of sight.

On the sidewalk lay a corpse, blooded from the silver cartridge exploding in the chest, another faceless victim to be identified only by the sharpened incisors and what was left of the clothing. Another vampyre leader executed. Another undesirable off the streets of this her Londinium. Another faction of this growing cult taken out and the members scattered to the four winds; the rich rubbing shoulders with the poor linked by a common goal now dissipated into the night sky to return to their chosen line of employment, lawyers, doctors, teachers, dock-hands, pick-pockets, ladies of the night. This new cult knew no boundaries only a unity in blood; that had spread onto the streets and into even polite society. Even during the daytime these few walked among the living, rich rubbing shoulders with the poor, soot churned by foot fall and the air thick with the toxic smell of carbon and coke.

Landing safely on the roof she peered over the parapet and smiled, following her ritual before returning to the office below, as if nothing had happened. Next time, which would be different as the sky-train was passing her building, or rather a halting stop was being set outside her building, outside her window.

She would need to rethink or change her career to something a little more mundane, a house-keeper, a governess perhaps or heaven forbid a homemaker and mother. As time went by she thought more and more about being that governess or housekeeper, settling down with a family or moving to the new world to ply her trade for a new master. But for now she had a second target in one day, a busy day. She crouched low behind the same wall, her mechanical wings folded flat. The same turbine bleaching warm air noisily muffling her slow steady approach to the edge of the roof and her decent to her quarry below.

She knew how to fly and her mechanical wings enabled her to stalk her prey easily and silently. At several thousand feet she looked just like a swallow-tailed bird of prey and that's how she liked it and that's how it remained until the passing of the division bell that heralded the dawn of a new century.

As she prepared, her same custom made '44 that held and fired six massive cartridges nestled safely in her tiny hands….it was time. With that she made her way to the edge, adjusted her brass goggles and jumped. With her target in squarely her sights she pulled the silent trigger. The massive projectile sped towards its intended recipient and as it did she pulled up, hung on the wind before finally disappearing out of sight. On the sidewalk lay another corpse, blooded from the cartridge exploding in the chest, another faceless victim to be identified only by the monogrammed pocket watch and what was left of the scarlet and ermine-trimmed clothing. This time a corrupt judge in the pay of the gangs had been executed, the sentence of death passed by a different judge, jury and executioner. One more unscrupulous undesirable off the sacred streets of her Londinium, one less to further taint the already tainted justice system of the land.

Returning safely to the roof she peered over the parapet and smiled, as the sky-train pulled into the platform several feet below her. Redressing she made her way down to the office and continued her work until the next card was slipped under the mat of her dwelling. Operations came up at a rate of one every month for the first year but then as they began to tail off she began to realise that it was time.

Time to hang up her wings only to be taken up by another as this time she was with a young child and hopefully someone able to pick up from whence she departed, whilst she faded into obscurity. As she turned away she whispered in to the wind "Tenna' ento lye omenta........quel kaima."

Writer's footnote – The Guild of Harpers is a fictional organization built up around the Forgotten Realms series produced for Dungeons and Dragons, the popular role-playing game.

Chapter Six - The Avenger – Londinium - 1875

The heavy black leaden studded door groaned on rusting hinges as it was forced asunder by the house-keeper. Their foot-prints clearing a path in the soot covered steps. No-one in years had used the front door of the foreboding white house; the drapes at the windows now yellowed or faded in the Victorian daylight. On the window mantels a thin layer of black soot crept over the wooded sashes and glass. Cobwebs formed homes to arachnids who took great delight in devouring the flies and other insects that crawled into the sticky traps.

Time had not been kind to the dwelling place and as the blackened light fell through the open portal and flooded into the large marbled hallway the condition on the inside did not fare much better but she was home; back in the Londinium family seat, her second love, although her heart ached to be back on that bleak and barren moor so many leagues away to the south west of this her Albion, her Wessex. Her Dartmoor, her Devon and above all her home.

But for now her time was required in the metropolis, she had reached the age where her inheritance was due to be paid from the estate of her dearly departed father. She had never married, not for the want of suitors but for the intent of keeping the funds her father had put into trust for her; intact. But she chose to wear purple in the lesser period of half mourning for her father who died some two and one-third years before. Her mother long since departing to the afterlife when she was but an angletwitch.

As she pondered the sight before her; a small white cat sidled alongside her, purring contentedly as if welcoming the mistress home shedding white fur over her purple crinoline bustle that flow down in a short train. The top nipped in at the waist was boned with shaped stays that restricted her movement but given the circumstances she wanted to give the air and grace that befitted her status as a *feme sole* having reached the legal age of twenty-one. Her hands and head covered in black, the four-button lace gloves protected her hands from the dust that covered the entrance hall and stairs of the town house. The small black silk hat perched forward with the lace vale covering her face.

Walking to the marble stairs she stopped at the low white wall and picked up the card that lay waiting for her return. She read the words and placed it in her matching bag before slowly climbing the staircase to the first floor and the one room she was not entitled to enter until now. Her father's study. The house keeper following after sorting the luggage in the grand hall.

It was her time to follow in her mother's footsteps but before she did she needed time to herself to re-acquaint herself with the Londinium family seat and the pressures and pleasures that brought. Opening the study door, what hit her foremost was the smell of pipe tobacco and whiskey, her father's only two vices, with exception of the volumes of books on shelves, each volume covered in a dust sheet and laid out in alphabetical order. On the large oak and ebony inlayed desk was a leather bound journal of cream velum with a unique crest, the same crest that her mother had shown her when she became of age. The Guild. Opening the book to a random page the curling script leapt of the page as she read out loud digesting the words. The words she knew as familiar, the words her father read to her when she was but a girl.

"The black stallion carried his Queen far into the night, the Saxon hordes swept over Albion and Arthur was gone but soon a king will come and the Sword of Avalon, the defender of Albion, the Excalibur will rise once more...but until that time she would claim it for her own.... she would be Queen, even but for a day of all Albion...

She would need Excalibur, returned to the mystic lake in the west...returned to the Lady of the Lake. Avalon… her Avalon, her home, one of the seven sisters... Excalibur would do her bidding, hers to wield, that great anmegil' in a world that was no longer sorglas, she had seen to that, neianor was over it was her time...the time of the Queen...run.

It was hrive and the ice was thick, the lake frozen, the air cold, all along the hills the fires of Beltane lit up the dark inky sky...the moon had not been seen since Arthur's death, perhaps this was an omen, perhaps darkness had descended upon the land, perhaps good will come to the land...only the Creator would know and that knowledge would naught be passed to such of the wizards of land. Merlin had gone...the old ways had gone...only she remained of the once noble house of Pendragon.

Pendragon, even the name in itself evokes passion but that was in the past and this was now...Morgana's time and the land would either bleed or heal under her rule. As she gathered pace towards the waters, the ice began to crack and the blade of kings rose from the black depths of that mystical place, her sceptred isle, her home."

The writing tailed off but she knew it was her father's hand that wrote those words. Flicking to another page she sat in the large leather chair and read

"The dark foreboding cathedral stood proud stretching into the night sky, the black lit by the silvery light of the first fruits of the full moon...the lunar days shorter as the winterfest approached...the light passing through the blackened stained windows onto the chancel steps outside...silence prevailed, a deathly silence...even the rats were absent.

Slowly the dark figure of a maiden approached the doors carrying a silver chalice, dripping with red liquid...was it wine...was it blood...only she knew and she had been this way before... time had been kind to her...she still had the freshness of youth... despite her age.

She was dressed in black, but not for mourning although her lover, her knight, her king had gone...dead to her...dying on a distant battlefield of time...gone forever. The corset tightly laced, the skirt flowing from the waist, full, made from the finest material known to beast and wode...she was..........beautiful...she had loved but would never love another...

Beneath the folds of skirt hid a stick, not a wooden object for walking but the stiletto blade of an assassin...thin, made from the toughest material known...razor sharp and clean. In her right laced up boot a long hat pin and on her horse...a longbow and anmegil, the original longsword, the Caliburn...sat on the saddle was a...an eagle...her familiar...her eodur...her love...on the back of the saddle was a box...a box containing two dwarven blades, finely balanced... mithril blades unsullied and moreover unbloodied in combat...

Around her neck two blackened silver Elven rings...with the inscription in an ancient tongue but in common speech "Out of friendship comes love" something neither would forget, the vows taken...entwined forever...the old ways.

Her red hair blacken in the dark...a grey streak hanging low be lying the truth of her real age...In the distance a cry of "to horse" and she was gone as quick as she came..."

Sleep took her as the quarter division bell rang heralding the star of a new day, the journal atop the bed sheets open, on a clean crisp vellum sheet, ready for her very own words, thoughts and sketches; keeping a tradition alive.

In the back pocket of the journal in the pocket were pictures she had drawn as a child that he had kept.

As daybreak rose she awoke from a weary slumber to the smell of freshly baked bread, bacon and eggs coupled with the distinct smell of ground coffee. The house-keeper had been busy, as there were no other staff in the house; each one, the butler, the footmen, the maids all being transferred to other noble houses when her father passed to the other side. Even her purple dress was laid out for her on the easy chair. Soon it would be time to relinquish the period of mourning but until that time came on the Feast of the Beheading on August 29 when the death of the saint is honoured, she would continue to observe Victorian customs. To her, her father was a saint although she also understood that her father in his jest and pagan beliefs would have rather the period of mourning be over by the summer solstice or the Feast of St John, at the very latest; so that she could enjoy the summer in fancy new clothes, rather than purple. But purple she chose to wear and wear it well for a further six months from arriving back in Londinium, thus avoiding the summer debutantes' ball and the court rigmarole that went into such stuffy depressing situations.

Dressing she hurried downstairs to the kitchen, welcoming breakfast on what would be a long day, however there was no breakfast laid out on the table even though for the last two and a half years she had eaten with the house-keeper in the kitchen of the cottage. Hurrying as best she could in the dress she made her way to the dining room where she found the house-keeper waiting to serve breakfast, usually the domain of a footman or butler. Breaking with all known protocol she invited the house-keeper to take table with her, not accepting the remonstrations. After the sumptuous spread together they cleared the table and made good before preparing for luncheon and the afternoons events that would take her into the hallowed walls and halls of the City of Londinium and her father's club. The Guild. The Guild of Harpers

Then in the year of our most Gracious Queen Victoria in her fifteenth year of mourning, Prince Albert having died in 1861 a shadow appeared on the south transept roof of St Paul's Cathedral. This was her first evening as the Avenger, the Assassin having long since retired to the Moor and the arms of a local country gentleman lawyer, her father. As she got used to the flimsier mechanical wings on her back bending and flexing, she pulled her brass goggles over her white-blonde hair. Pushing the wings into the lock position she stepped off the building, narrowly missing the sky-train pulling out of the terminus below her. She fell, headfirst, the wind rushing over the wings allowing her to plummet to the ground and certain death in the black soot filled smog of Londinium.

Her oversized custom made Derringer that held and fired six massive cartridges nestled safely in her tiny hands. The stock and hammer from a normal Army issue Colt 44 accurately propelled the shot towards the intended, the only difference was the six barrels as opposed to a single barrel. This modification was to vary the striations on the shell casing rendering them untraceable or causing a delay in traceability.

Getting her head around the initial adrenalin rush of free-falling, she gradually pushed her arms back allowing the wings to level off parallel to the ground, before that certain snap as the updraft took over and she flew. She flew allowing the thermals to carry her back towards the roof of her building and a safe landing. That was enough for the first day although she noted that it would take practice and time to fly. Time that she did not have as her first assignment was on the final countback with only seventy-two hours left on the clock.

The target for her first “hit” was a “well-known” male relative of the notorious Sir Francis Dashwood, the 18th Century founding father of the equally notorious “Hellfire Club” and a static hit; not flight involved; the Guild making certain she had the stomach for the work that she would be entrusted to undertake. The relative was had been re-inventing the perverted practices of Sir Francis Dashwood for the wealthy Victorian gentleman, hell-bent on self-gratification and pleasure and political gain. She knew who her target was, having been introduced during a high-society ball that her employer had instructed or rather ordered her to attend earlier in the week at the club. Her target was lean, muscular and handsome to a point of being too perfect. Not that they hit it off, not only was he trying to be *that* perfect but he was also completely pompous and utter flash shite. Normally she would not know her target but this time she took great delight in pulling the trigger twice, allowing two cartridges to disrupt the intended recipient and ending his life. Another undesirable, another purveyor of everything that was opposite to the natural world laying on the side walk, his chest cavity opened, the contents washing the black dirty pavements crimson; as he fell. Dead.

She took her vocation personally, just as the Assassin had done years before, partly because she had a job to do and secondly she had to live up to her mother's reputation. She was a second generation Harper that she knew of. Many more "hits" or assignments came and went; each one perfected and executed in the timely fashion, befitting an agent of the Crown. With each assignment it became easier and quicker but that ease came at a price. And that price could have been her own sanity, only saved by the secretariat job she had in the same firm as her mother, although they now had the new front striking Daugherty Visible which was introduced in 1893, encompassing the familiar four banks of keys. This allowed her to see the work much clearer and accurately rather that the old fashioned upward striking keys. Progress on every level but that meant working harder and smarter; not that she minded as the hard work did not bother her.

The Harper gathered her belongings from the roof-top hiding place and hurriedly got ready to fly. Her secret had almost been discovered and so she needed a new place to hide, a sanctuary. Only this time someplace higher than her place of work and close to her new office at the Inner Temple. Her site, her site was consecrated as the Church of The Blessed Virgin Mary or more commonly known as the Temple Church, the once home of the Knights Templar, the circle church.

As she stood in the hallowed circular space, she bowed her head allowing the overwhelming sense of something or someone wash over her. As she closed her eyes, she saw the past, a past over 800 years ago but as clear as she was standing there. Trying to gain her composure as the vision passed she took her journal, the same one her father and mother had kept and opened it to a random page that illuminated under the gloomy sunlight that fell through the windows and into the circular transept. Looking at the open page she read the words aloud as if drawn by the surroundings, although the title seemed a little wrong.

The Monster

There was no grand ceremony, no banner waving, no-one to wave him off as he set out on this crusade…only himself and his great sword…the journey would be arduous and without mercy with many demons to conquer but conquer them he must…his own soul depended on it…nee demanded it…cleansing…

Beside the words was a sketch of a long sword, presumably one carried into battle, the same on that now hung in her father's study on the wall by the window. The only piece missing would have been the Crusader's side arm, a short dagger fashioned identically to the long sword. As she stared at the words her mind filled with pictures of those events. Allowing the vison to settle and turning to a fresh page in the book she too began to write in a flowing cursive script using aged brown ink on cream velum what she had seen.

"Facing the enemy square the robed knights drew their swords, not a simple short sword carried by a foot soldier but a great long sword, rolled and forged, each sword finished with a silver cross shaped pommel…significant in its meaning…. revered by the few, feared by the many… Their swift but heavy horses stood beside them, as their riders taking their swords in their right hand, their chainmail hauberk and coif shimmering in the noon-day sun, their once white robes, muddied and torn after the previous encounters, knelt in prayer to their Creator. The battle for the Holy Land would be swift and decisive…"

Alone with her thoughts of history, her concentration only broken by the twin organs of the church practicing for the services that Sunday and a rag-tag procession of choristers making their way to the chancel under the direction of Dr Edward John Hopkins, barking orders and instructions from the organ loft. Time for her to leave and return to the day-time job not far from the church and to the grind-stone and monotony of life. Soon it would be time for her to hang up her wings only to be taken up by another as this time she was with child, a child she could impart her knowledge to and hopefully someone able to pick up from whence she departed, fading into obscurity. Returning to Armanathian and the peace and tranquillity that that green and pleasant land brought to raise her child with her husband and their familiar.

Chapter Eight – A new life, a new beginning

The new tree of all trees from which the first crop came was dying and with it the land that had been scoured and scorched by rogue dragon's breath. The world white with ash, the charred remains of the once great kingdom; now just a forgotten realm. In the distance the harvest fires had almost extinguished themselves, the Beltane fires long since gone out as the season of winterfest dawned and the promise of snow. The old ways gone and with it the once green and pleasant lands, home, Albion, her love.

A lone grey wolf with mechanical back legs dragged a white form for the last remaining miles to the sacred tree. There was no horse in sight, that had been eaten on route and now the wolf's white coat was stained red by its last meal. This time there was no shadow overhead just the grey overhanging sky, the sun long since departed from the land.

Why had the land become so infected with a sweeping sickness that turned everything it touched? This bode the question who was left to save them and why was this the last sacred apple. This time there was no serpent in the Garden of Eden This time it was her decision and hers alone for the making. Sending her wolf away for just a while, she took the apple allowing the tree to wither and die. Taking a bite, she lay in the soft black as the grey snow covered ground to wait for the inevitable; the remains of the apple beside her. Whilst from her side a black clockwork spider scuttled from the scene safely to its layer dragging with it her leather necklace on which hung Tekil'loki e' kuu…

On the hill by the now ruined church overlooking the derelict cottage a lone wolf with mechanical back legs howled at the moon that appeared in the low horizon. It's song a lament to the fallen, a lament to the dying, a lament to his beloved. Then complete silence. Faraway in a different land the emerald stone in her headpiece began to glow dimly; the emerald in the white birch staff glowed in unison. One word entered her head. Morchiant.

Although she was not scared, she had faced dark shapes before and come out on top, the great creator saw to that and normally this time it would be no different. She turned from the river and mounted her horse and with a valiant cry of "a roch" the dappled white stallion sped through the forest twisting and turning, a blur of grey and white light following the meandering course of the river. Its source so many leagues into the hills in the distance. The wind in her dark brown hair, her flowing silver gown trailing in the wake created, flowing out behind the stallion's tail, changing colours in the light. Her Anmegil was hanging from the saddle across her left side, the staff ever present in her left hand. She knew that soon it would be time but for now her own safety, her own preservation even was uppermost in her mind.

She had never run from a fight before but today was different, today was not a good day for one of such exquisite beauty to get the blood of her foes on her hands or even her dress, today was her day it was the meeting of the sun and the moon in the west. It was Yéni and Loa at the same time, a time of beauty and magic reborn. As she turned away she whispered as her mother had done all those years before into the wind "Tenna' ento lye omenta........quel kaima."

Chapter Nine - The Dawn, March and Death of the Spiders – Londinium 1886

The work bench was saturated with mechanical bits and bobs, cogs, springs small match like pieces of brass, fob watches, many without hands and papers; technical papers. The mess that was the life blood of the engineer. Cast aside by his own family and shunned in later years by humanity, the old man with bent fingers created, first one then two and before long a whole line of small brass spiders each one no bigger than a cricket ball but each one lovingly hand-crafted. If he had the inclination he would name each of them but that was not his nature nor were they his children, he just created mechanical toys for children; his usual toy was the common monkey with two cymbals that loudly clapped when wound up, much to the annoyance of the parents who would write to him to complain that once wound up the monkey would take an age to wind itself down and become quiet again.

It was those people that had been his undoing and the reason why he now made what he made. Being the toymaker he had a premises in High Holborn opposite the now closed "Noah's Ark", the toy shop opened in 1760 before moving to its present location in Regents Street in 1881. Business in those days was brisk because he catered for the more obscura clientele. Those to each he would send a clockwork spider in the first instance before saturating the Metropolitan and county boroughs of the land. An infestation of mechanical spiders. On his work bench sat a copy of the 1885 revised version of the Bible, a little tatty for a new edition; opened to Exodus 10 where in what looked like thin oil the thirteenth verse had been high-lighted "And Moses stretched forth his rod over the land of Egypt, and the Lord brought an east wind upon the land that day; and all night and when it was morning, the east wind brought the locusts"

It was time, for they shall cover the face of the whole of the earth, so that the land was darkened, and the wicked shall perish.

Across the dark foreboding nee satanic town of Londinium 1886, the high court circuit judge sat by the fire in the tatty old Chesterfield, his cigar and glass of malt nestled quietly on the small table next to him. On the floor beside him the Illustrated London News lay entwined with the Daily Telegraph; research one could suppose in readiness for the Michaelmass quarter session at the Bailey. A coal fire was spitting and whistling to itself; the gas fusion bulbs growling dimly, he watched cautiously as the clockwork spider slowly paced the floor…it's tightly wound spring winding down until with a jolt it stopped, completely devoid of all power and life…with all the care of a new born child he gathered it up and re-wound small the brass key before returning it to the floor to set off on its travels. No emotion just the desire to move, like all clockwork toys.

Tick, tick, tick…not the tick-tock of the mantel clock high above the fire but the tick, tick, tick of a steady eight beat tattoo on the wooden floor.

The motor began to spring into life and the spider began to place one foot in front of the other, a little wobbly at first but then all eight legs working in harmony heading towards the door but first the obstacles. The heavily polished wood grain gave no traction. Sliding it made its way to the thick Victorian rug and certain freedom. Its clockwork spring slowing the movement whilst in the chair the occupant slumped, his face turning ashen and a small trickle of blood running down his thumb, dropping onto the floor. The spider gone its job had been done. Baker Street was quiet again until the break of dawn.

Meanwhile north in the smoky industrial metropolis of Manchester, she slept, her dreams kept her tossing and turning all night long, the rem sleep that she craved had gone and she was left staring into the inky blackness of the night sky. The lights in the street long since extinguished.

The same tick, tick, tick…only this time not the quiet tick of her brass and glass encased carriage clock.

The motor having been quiet for most of the journey suddenly began to spring into life and the spider began to steadfastly place one foot in front of the other, eight legs working in harmony bearing an eight note tune heading towards the bed…the same type of eight-legged clockwork spider that crept, silently crept, murderously crept.

The small pocket watch that made up the back of the mechanical wonder rang, all four tones in E major that made up the Westminster chime; quietly at first and then broadcast to the nation. Startled she sat up and looked down to the wooden floor upon which the bed sat. There it stood motionless, its fake eyes pleading with her to be wound up again.

Carefully she lifted the automaton and wound the small brass key protruding from the side before placing it back on the floor. The spider paused and then scuttled away and the occupant slumped half on the bed and half on the floor, her face turning ashen. The spider gone, another victim; blood dripping from her little finger soaking into the wooden floor.

North of the border a spider wound its way down a silken thread and onto the copper taps of the enameled bath. The water riding up to the overflow; the boiler over the bath heating the water bleaching black smoke into the dark Edinburgh sky. The gas lights emitting an eerie luke-warm glow as the rain fell from black clouds in a blackened sky.

The two young wards sat at either end of the enameled bath, while nanny was busying herself with other tasks, her eyes averted, her hands laying the towels over the newly installed oil fueled heated towel rail. The spider ticked as the silken thread detached itself, almost remotely from the body, allowing the spider to slide into the bath and climb out the other side and scuttle across the floor and out of the open door. Slowly the two young wards slipped under the surface of the bubbling hot water, their faces bulbous and ashen and then blue. The only marks to distinguish foul play was a small single puncture in the small of each of their lower backs

In front of the tub now devoid of all sound the nanny continuing to busy herself, lost in her dreams and now having lost her charges and her credibility to work.

Far, far away from the smoky north back in the Metropolis of Londinium the full moon weakly lit up the night sky, the smog from the steam and coal put paid to any brilliance that had been before, the man in the moon was now frowning rather than the smile that previous centuries had seen. A perfect night for hunting and being hunted, in the distance the bell of the great Tower of Westminster chimed twelve times, the dawn of a new day and a frenzy of activity below.

A body had been found in the Docklands area with a single puncture wound in the neck and a small trail of blood congealed in a straight line down the deck, pooling on the floor. But this was no ordinary killing this was a dead vampire, not turned to ash like all the others…this was something new…something strange…

The Police were baffled not knowing which way to turn. Nothing like this had happened before, certainly not to a vampire. There were no defensive wounds and no blood around the mouth so this vampire had not fed but had been fed upon. The Police surgeon looked closely at the wound, the small puncture wound was tinged with a silver ring, the same silver ring that they had seen before. The Police knew they had a serial killer or something on their hands but did not know whom or even what was causing these random acts of malice, maybe time would tell or moreover maybe it would be confined to files marked unsolved until the end of time.

The newly establish Daily Mail cemented its vulgar lower middle class reputation by printing the banner headline "Four victims in as many days; related or a coincidence?" with the sub-text of another unsolved Jack-the-Ripper case or just incidents of random un-related events with the words Police baffled below the picture of the latest posed victim.

At the same time in the county borough of Plymouth, as the Dreadnaught fleet docked alongside the quays at HMNB Devonport, the servicemen's playground began to fill and with it the number of servicemen going AWOL from either ship or barracks as the invasion of servicemen was surpassed by the invasion of clockwork spiders. Although only a few were to take a victim as too many would cast suspicion on the two rival services pitching an all-out war, although no love was lost between the Navy based at HMS

Vivid shore establishment and those on active or shore leave deployment from the Devonport Flotilla. Civilians knew to stay away from the area and takings suffered at the New Palace Theatre of Varieties on the corner of Union Street and Phoenix Street, however the economy from the drinking establishments increased, both benefitting the area and the corporation.

Slowly the number of bodies piled high behind the Theatre, it would be days before someone checked as the building was shut for the duration of the homecoming. Each victim killed by a single silver-ringed puncture wound, each victim a victim of his own drunken curiosity following the small clockwork spider to the rear where another dangled from a sliver of silver thread laying claim to the living. Every so often the spiders changed rolls and one became the prey or rather the catalyst and the other the assassin but they always worked together becoming more and more dependent unlike the previous killing which were done by an independent spider.

It was almost as if they had a hive or pack mentality driving them ever forward. An assault on the much fabricated existence of the planet. As the hive left and headed toward the coastal path and the open ocean, a tract of verse caught the wind of eight legs and flew into the night sky before being blown to the window of the local gentleman's club, the verse was the same Exodus 10 verse, hewn from a Bible that one of the servicemen had dropped. "And Moses stretched forth his rod over the land of Egypt, and the Lord brought an east wind upon the land that day; and all night and when it was morning, the east wind brought the locusts". The verse covered in oil, the same lubricating oil.

On the back of the paper the haunting words of Romans 12 verses 17- 19. "Render to no man evil for evil. Take thought for things honourable in the sight of all me. If it be possible, as much as in you lieth, be at peace with all men. Vengeance belongeth unto me"

Then suddenly just as fast as the hive killing spree had started it was over, in each metropolitan city or town where the small mechanical spiders had stalked and hunted, they were beginning to appear on the street. Individuals drawn together like lemmings ready for one last jump but this time as the assembly of spiders gathered they appeared different completely wound-down, devoid of motion as if dead. As if the hand or hands that fed them had forgotten to wind the keys, their tightly coiled spring now no more than a circle or strip of oil tainted brass, as if bleeding.

Just a faint ticking came from the underside of the meticulously built clockwork then silence, as people began to stamp on the spiders, obliterating them from the face of the cursed earth to dust from whence they came by the hand of someone, an engineer. A skilled engineer with a grudge against humanity or certain types of humanity. Who and what no-one would know, each spider meticulously hand-made without tool marks or signature each one individually crafted and now each one potentially dying, silently and almost reverently.

Back in Londinium in the middle of Abney Park, one of the magnificent seven parkland cemeteries opened in the early reign of Queen Victoria, close to Church Street and the tomb of William and Catherine Booth, the founders of the Salvation Army a mausoleum door had been prised open. The cobwebs wrenched from their holdings. In the gloom of the marble monstrosity a small clockwork spider scuttled down the steps and paused. A small almost burnt out candle revealed his, her or rather its master hanging by a rope, his feet teetering on the edge of the stool, his tools all around him. His reign of terror now coming to an end as more and more spiders gathered. No note was left as to the reasons why or how or whom but it was as if the magic had gone from those infernal creatures as they either lay dying or climbing the body of their creator eventually covering him in brass, cogs and gears.

As they climbed upwards in haste the rickety old stool slipped and carried away on a tide of clockwork movement and with a sickening snap the engineer fell, his neck broken; dislodging a number of his creation who scampered back up his body, placing more and more weight on the rope until he was engulfed in his own creative misgivings. No remorse, no forgiveness just dead and forgotten.

Outside a swirling gale blew up, scattering leaves to the four corners of the cemetery before heading directly towards the doors; blowing on either side like to hands clasping the handles. Then with a resonant crash lounder than a clap of thunder the doors closed; the blackened rain that followed soaked the earth allowing vines to hastily grow sealing its secret with sinewy branches, forever. Opposite on the neatly manicured lawn a small object peered from behind a small grave marker before burying safely itself into the ground to wait out its days.

High in the canopy of the sprawling oak trees that surrounded the graves, catacombs and mausoleums sat a flight of small mechanical dragons each one with a small engraved fob watch ticking. Sensitive prying eyes watching and waiting.

Despite the chaos, death and destruction this did not need the involvement of the family as the toymaker's own pitiful creation brought about his downfall and his tomb was sealed never to be reopened.

Chapter Ten - The Aviator - Sutton - 1898

The newly subscription built Promenade Pier jutted out of the land like a carbuncle of steel engineering but it was the norm. A feat of late Victorian engineering. A band-stand and promenade for the sprawling populous living and migrating to the Port of Plymouth.

The band-stand was silent and the pier was empty save a lone female figure with heavy gossamer wings out-stretched as if ready to fly. Not that man knew how to fly or so they believed. Icarus having had his wings burnt several millennia before and his tale now confined to the stories parents and teachers tell children. Taking hold of the wooden super-structure she drew them to her side, the wings and wood now looking like a boned bustle that would have been worn years before. There was no derringer, Colt 44 or 45 strapped to her leg, just a small knife and a compass shaped aviator bag attached to her waist. Although the bag bore a remarkable and similar logo.

A contemporised writer wrote the following description about the Pier

"It is one of the latest additions to the many attractions of Plymouth and is one of the finest structures of the kind on the coast, its total length being 480 feet. On the pier head is erected a handsome windscreen, enclosing a space 120 ft. by 109 ft. in which the bandstand is erected, also a large number of reserved chairs for the use of visitors not wishing to promenade during the concerts which are its chief attraction, the Royal Marine and other Military Bands, which it is the good fortune of Plymouth to have stationed in her midst, performing frequently.

In providing good landing accommodation for all kinds of vessels at any time of tide, the Pier has supplied a long-felt want, and it is anticipated that yachting at the port will receive quite an impetus, not that the cause of complaints in this respect has been removed.

We must refer visitors to the time bills for particulars of the large number of pleasure steamers leaving the Pier, for the enjoyable water excursions to the celebrated Eddystone Lighthouse, up the River Tamar, and other rivers, all of which are well worth a visit."

As she walked along the pier she heard the familiar sounds of the steamer returning to the far end of the pier, having taken its charges for a tour of the Eddystone Breakwater and newer lighthouse through the large ironclad cruisers and lesser naval vessles moored in the Sound awaiting either orders to sale to far off destinations defending Queen Victoria's empire or awaiting entrance to the dockyard for refit, upgrade or breaking. The original Smeaton built lighthouse was erected on the Eddystone reef in 1759 at a cost of £40,000, but when it was discovered that the sea was undermining the rock it was standing on the decision came to remove it brick by brick in 1880 and the years thereafter. Although only two-thirds of the superstructure was rebuilt on the top of Plymouth Hoe, its seventy-two-foot structure bearing down on the pier. As she came off the pier she ensured that her wings had formed the perfect bustle so she would not draw attention to herself in the sparsely populated street. Sparsely populated was right; for it was Matins times and every God fearing person was either in chapel or at the parish church of St Andrew in the centre of the town to listen to the choir (under the tutelage of Dr Harry Moreton, Director of Music who was appointed in 1885), rather than the sermon of the day which was probably full of worries and wows as a new century dawned.

The smell of fish hit her squarely, cutting the back of her nose and throat making her retch but she kept going. The fishing fleet had returned and were unloading their catch of the day. Even on a Sunday the fleet sailed and landed when the tides were right. And usually the full moon and high spring tides brought a good catch. Although the full moon and spring tides did render the vessels closer to the quay liable to beach on the quay until they could be either re-floated or pushed into the water. Hurrying along the coastal road towards the steps where the pilgrim fathers set sail for the new world in September 1620 and where the prisoner Napolean Bonaparte was supposed to have set foot in 1815, whilst being held on HMS Bellerophon before being exiled to St Helena in the South Atlantic. She turned into New Street and the Elizabethan House that was now stood empty but due to be demolished, thus wiping out three hundred and fifty plus years of history. A black dog rushed passed her and disappeared at the corner of The Barbican near the fish quay. She shivered fearing that the beast was a wishthound, a ghostly or haunted beast. But her fears were unfounded as a voice in front of her called for the beast as the owner turned down White Lane towards South-side Street. Too many late nights and too many ancient folk tales that were springing up towards the end of the century, especially with the Victorian fascination for all things macabre, gothic and supernatural. And being so close to both the sea and the Moor those legends were overly exacerbated for the grockles.

As she opened the front door she noticed a letter on the mat embossed with a seal that she had not seen for several years. Not since her mother had stopped taking to the wing had she seen the Harp and Crescent Moon. Carefully closing the door without allowing the hinges to whine under the stresses, she made her way to what would have been the scullery at the rear of the dwelling. Pouring herself a drink from the jug she opened the letter and digested the contents. It was her time to take over the reins, not as an Assassin nor an Avenger but an Aviator. Peace had broken out in the land and the Guild of Harpers were now a service attached to the monarch's personal bodyguard, moreover a covert message service between royalty in both the Empire and the Continent. A covert message service for the monarch? Was there really that much unrest outside the waters of her Albion. She re-read the letter before folding it into the pleats of her skirt. One more sleep before reporting to the fortification of St Michael and then St Nicholas Island before being renamed in the sixteenth century as Drake's Island which would be her home for the next few years. After laying out her meagre things she lay her head on the makeshift cot that had become her bed, her stiletto under the pillow as it had been every night for whatever sleep would come her way.

As the dawn rose over the town in the East she gathered her belongings into her messenger bag and left the comfort of the old house to begin life on a fortified island. She would gain passage on one of the supply vessels that took provisions to the company of artillerymen station on the island. From the jetty of she could see the three new quick-fire guns on the casement battery, remembering that they had only been installed to replace the heavier 9-inch 12 ton RML guns, on the eastern side of the Island. These 21 guns that formed the casemated battery where the same as the primary guns on the ever-familiar fleet of smaller ironclad battleships and secondary guns on the larger ironclads until they were decommissioned and turned into supply vessels. The island itself was one of the principal defenses to the city of Plymouth, the others being the breakwater fort with its fourteen 12.5-inch and four 10-inch rifled muzzle-loading guns in armoured casemates which were armed in 1879. Devils Point, Eastern and Western King and the newer Penlee and Garden batteries on the Cornish side of the Tamar at Mount Edgecombe. Thus guarding the approaches to the dockyard at Devonport, just a few miles up the Tamar estuary to the west of town centre. The only contact without using transport to shore was the telegraph cable link to Mount Batten.

As the small coal-fired tramp steamer pulled out of Sutton harbour she bade farewell to her home, knowing she would not see it for some time or at least not to visit. Her duty was now to the Monarch and defense of the realm. Naught would come between her and her duty as it never did. Sitting in the bow of the vessel she opened her bag and pulled out a leather necklace on which hung Tekil'loki e' kuu, placing it on her neck it felt like an old friend. A comfort passed from generation to generation throughout the years. If she could look down upon the ship she would clearly make out the silhouette of a dragon beneath the steamer. As the tramp steamer passed through the invisible deep water channel toward the leeward side of the island and the stone jetty it pointed its nose eastwards toward Staddon Heights with its casements, jetty and pier and recently furnished with two 12.5" RML's with the main purpose of bombarding hostile invaders to this green and pleasant land. The Staddon Heights Battery complementing the Maker Battery, on the Western (opposite) side of the Sound and the imposing Breakwater fort some one hundred yards from the breakwater.

Disembarking as the steamer held fast against the jetty she looked up at the formidable backside of the Elizabethan complex that she would be calling home for the next few years; or until she was able to hang up her wings and retire or even for better or for worse marry and have children she could call her own. Climbing the steps on the leeward side of the island she made her way to the garrison commanders office and introduced herself, as if reporting for duty. After the pleasantries were exchanged, the commander's adjutant showed her to her quarters, her home for the foreseeable future; a rather sparse largish room in the old Napoleonic era barracks. The room however was on the top floor with two windows overlooking the sound but had no running mains fed water and very basic plumbing, but it was hers.

The days on the fortified island grew longer and the journeys even more so, by the time her third tour had begun she was already flying to Londinium and back at least twice a week, maybe more. Although the flight still excited her in principle, the thought of dodging increasingly more dirigibles hanging over the sky did not.

Still she flew, carried on the thermals of warm air created by the cities, Plymouth, Exeter, Bristol, Reading and then into Londinium, basically following the Great Western Railway built by Brunel many years before. In fact, when she got too tired or the thermals dropped she could easily and silently land on top of one of the covered carriages and ride the steam locomotive, remembering to flatten herself on the approach to many of the tunnels that carved their ways through Wessex and on to the metropolis. The terminus at Paddington having been opened some sixty years before and then upgraded a little over forty into the vast expanse of brick and steel it is now served as a landmark for her flight in from Reading some 40 miles away. This was the difficult leg as the updraft of thermals was stronger here due to the increased populous and the requirement for coal or coke fired appliances. Even this far south and west of the metropolis industry was squeezed into a tight area, everyone competing for space and productivity.

From Paddington she knew it was only a short flight or longer walk to the offices in Lincoln's Inn, the heady home of justice and the founding seat of the Knights Templar, now the home of her organisation. A day spent in the smoke did nothing for her and rather than suffer the slings and arrows of the evening skies out of the metropolis she took the evening train from Paddington to Plymouth and then glide her way back to the island under the cover of the moon from the top of Saltash Road. Eventually every week was the same, one day up, one day in the metropolis, then back by train, finally one day of rest and then repeat. Her days in

Londinium where monotonous, acting as a foot messenger during the day, carrying messages between the Guild and the Monarch's private secretary, just a glorified runner. Although the evenings would be slightly more entertaining. Even then on her days off, if urgent messages were required to be taken then it would be no rest day until the end of the month; when she would have a whole weekend free, albeit grounded to remain on the island. Those whole weekends flew by when they happened as there was so much to explore on that small outcrop on the approaches to her city or time just to sit and watch the world go by or sleep, which was the usual pattern of events. This happened for weeks on end, the only company she knew was when she wore her pendant was her loki, her protector who was with her for the duration of the flight, particularly when the cloud cover was dense and low as it was becoming with the fervent use of coal.

And on those slack days she could be called upon to make a short hop either early day-break or late into the even-tide to the now heavily fortified Breakwater Fort, with its 140 service men packed into a concrete oval encased in the rock sea bed some six fathoms down. (36 feet or just over 10 metres) and just over 12,750 sq ft (1,184m^2) surface area; to drop messages to the garrison commander who was effectively cut off from all civilisation during rotation except by semaphore and search-light and when both of those went down via old fashioned flag waving.

Finally, on the eve of Beltane and the lighting of the line of bonfires along the coast to signify the period of time, it was time to hang up her tired and world weary wings forever, her duty had come to an end as she had had enough. Usually the first borne child normally took up the reigns and became the new Aviator but she had no first child only a second child, a special gift. Silently she climbed aboard the same tatty tramp steamer on its return journey with her meagre belongings and sat in the stern atop a box of something. As the steamer pulled away she turned and whispered as both her mother and grandmother had done all those years before into the wind "Tenna' ento lye omenta........quel kaima" adding the words Slainte mhor agus a h-uile beannachd duibh". [1]

Writer's footnote - The superstructure of the pier was destroyed by German bombing in 1942. In 1952, the last traces of the Pier, including the underwater supports, were demolished at the expense of the War Damage Commission and Plymouth Promenade Pier disappeared for ever.

Writer's footnote – The Parish Church of St Andrew has stood in the same place since the first strains of Christian Worship in the 8th Century before the first Saxon Church was established and taken under control of the Priory of Plympton until its dissolution n 1538. Various works of restoration and rebuild and additions took place over the next several centuries until on night in 1941 the Church was hit during the blitz over Plymouth and two years later in 1943 became a garden church until 1949 when re-building work took place and the building re-consecrated in 1957, one year before the said Dr Harry Moreton retired.

In the now famous picture of the Garden Church taken from the tower, the depleted but robed choir who lead the worship had six ladies singing, one of whom is a relative of the writer and approximately 40 years later the writer stood in exactly the spot as a chorister from 1979 – 1988, when Londinium called, however the writer has never formally resigned from the choir and may still be considered a member.

Writer's footnote - 1 "Good health and every good blessing to you!"

The End - Epilogue

At what seemed to be the end of days, it came to pass that the Guild of Harpers were once again confined to the annuls of history and with that she, the last operative, like her predecessors went about trying to build a normal life. Although she was still haunted by what she had seen and done, those faces and the faces of her mother's and grandmother's targets that would always be firmly etched on her sub-conscious mind. The ones whose lives she ended, her mother ended and her grandmother ended over the course of over half a century of service.

Now fast approaching her older years, she updated her faded leather bound journal for one last time before wrapping it in brown paper and string and sending it to Governor of Dartmoor Prison to place in the white room of the white cottage. The cottage that was just outside the prison, guarded by her loki, which was overlooked by the rebuilt thirteenth century Church of St Michael de Rupe. [1] Her heart ached as she missed her younger daughter and her husband, her lover. Her cottage on the Moor now just an empty shell, save the collection of leather bound journals; her younger daughter having left and moved to Londinium and her husband's last letter from those foreign climates was a one-line letter, not even signed with the usual ending which left her cold to the core. The words she would remember forever. "I saw our eldest daughter today and she was calling to me"

Five days later she received a single telegram from the War Office trimmed with black and a further letter from her husband repeating the haunting words of his last letter home. She knew that this was the end and so despairingly she gathered a single rose from the luscious garden and walked barefoot to Armanthian where she lay at the foot of the remaining steps to the hallowed but ruined great hall of Armanthian, her family seat. Her husband had gone, taken on some distant battlefield in a war to protect the country's sovereignty. Clutching the single red rose she curled her wings around herself and drifted into a haunted sleep whilst far off, whistles blew. Zero hour. The date was the first day of July in the year of our Creator one thousand, nine hundred and sixteen. A day that would be remembered as some far off muddy field.

Postscript

At the dawn of the 21st Century, the once great British Empire was no more. The Commonwealth of counties that remained loyal to the crown was ever diminishing that had shrunk to only sixteen countries voluntarily sharing our Monarch. The United Kingdom was no longer united in a common cause and power had been devolved from Parliament in Londinium to regional parliaments or assemblies. But what of this great nation, we survived for centuries by standing on our own two feet, held an Empire together during the reign of our second longest serving Monarch and fought most of the members of this social club called Europe and won and are still winning albeit in peaceful times against an unseen enemy.

Invaders came and went…the Dinosaurs, the Ice Age, the Romans, The Picts, The Norsemen, The Normans and even in 1940 the Saxons tried again but the spirit of the Country prevailed. To paraphrase a quote "An' we drummed them up the channel as we drummed them long ago." [2] History can be re-written but soon the paper pages will close and a sword will rise once more."

Writers Footnote

1. For the sake of this and other stories The Church and Prison are in close proximity, whereas actually they are about 10 miles apart across some most in-hospitable mires and Tors. Again there is no cottage situate in a valley outside the prison as the prison is surrounded by the same mires on three of the four sides.

[12]"Take my drum to England, hang et by the shore, Strike et when your powder's runnin' low; If the Dons sight Devon, I'll quit the port o' Heaven, An' drum them up the Channel as we drummed them long ago." — From "Drake's Drum" by Sir Henry Newbolt in 1897...According to legend a drum owned by Sir Francis Drake will beat in times of national crisis and the spirit of Drake will return to aid his country. The original drum being housed in Drake's home of Buckland Abbey, just outside the historic city of Plymouth on the moor.

Hic est Excalibur, gladium, et reges Avalon. [1]

The hunter homeward speeds in haste,
Ere fogs o'ertake him on the waste;
And if to Foxtor mires he roam,
He'll bid a long adieu to home;
A dreary shroud is o'er his head,
A yawning swamp around him spread;
Spell-bound and lost he ventures on
One fatal step – and all is done;
Hopeless he struggles, vain his throes,
Deeper and deeper down he goes!
The raven claps her ebon wing,
His dirge the howling winds may sing,
And mists will spread the last sad pall
O'er that dark grave unknown to all".

© Dartmoor Days – Edward William Lewis Davis – 1863

Writers footnote -1 Here is Excalibur, the sword of kings and Avalon.

About the Writer and acknowledgements

I am a fifty-something Devonian and father to two beautiful girls (one of whom was taken very young), living on the edge of the Moor, having recently returned from Londinium.

By day I am a Lawyer specialising in Succession and by night a Musician and Writer.

I would like to thank firstly my wife and daughter for putting up with me while I write.

I would also like to thank several people for helping to push this in the right direction and giving me the inspiration, you know who you are, so I won't embarrass you further.

Any finally thank you dear reader for taking the trouble to buy this little novella and please do not forget to leave a review.

For further details please contact me at
foxtorpublishing@outlook.com

For cover/illustrative enquires please contact Bex Sutton at
bex@primalst.com

www.ingramcontent.com/pod-product-compliance
Lightning Source LLC
Chambersburg PA
CBHW030415310726
48979CB00002B/420

* 9 7 8 1 7 3 9 9 1 7 2 1 0 *